This igloo book belongs to:

George
···

Contents

igloobooks

Published in 2023
First published in the UK by Igloo Books Ltd
An imprint of Igloo Books Ltd
Cottage Farm, NN6 0BJ, UK
Owned by Bonnier Books
Sveavägen 56, Stockholm, Sweden
www.igloobooks.com

0423 005
4 6 8 10 9 7 5
ISBN 978-1-80368-034-7

Written by Lindsey Dean
Illustrated by Lizzy Doyle

Designed by Alice Dainty
Edited by Daisy Edwards

Printed and manufactured in China

Five-Minute STORIES FOR 3 YEAR OLDS

igloobooks

Arun's Special Day

Arun woke up with a big YAWN.
He raced downstairs, but someone was missing.

Where was Mummy?
Lindy the babysitter
was there instead.

Shall we go to the
playground together
after breakfast?

asked Lindy.

Then, Arun remembered. Mummy wouldn't be there all day because she had a brand-new job to go to. So, Lindy took him to the playground instead!

But Mummy still wasn't home when they got back.

Later, when he heard footsteps coming up the path, Arun ran to the front door.

He was so pleased to have her back that he held on tightly to her until she tucked him into bed.

But when Arun woke up in the morning,
Mummy was gone again, and Lindy was back!

She handed Arun
his favourite T-Rex,
but he didn't want to
play dinos with Lindy.
He wanted Mummy!
So, he threw the T-Rex
on the floor and
it broke in two.

CRACK!

Arun was sure Mummy would be cross,
but she gave him a great big cuddle at bedtime.

It's okay to be sad
when I'm not here.
But you can still have
fun with Lindy as well.

The next morning, Arun woke up to the smell of something delicious.

This time, he knew Mummy wouldn't be there, but he raced downstairs and into the kitchen where Lindy was making something special.

Then, Lindy had another surprise.
They were going to...

DINO LAND!

This is so much fun!

Lindy even bought him a brand-new T-Rex, and they played
dinos together all afternoon until Mummy came home.

The Rainy Day Picnic

Daddy was going to take Sophie out for a picnic.
She had the perfect new hat, and she couldn't
wait to wear it for their special outing.

Daddy even promised to pack all her favourite treats.

When Sophie ran downstairs to make sure her fairy cakes were in the picnic basket, she heard a very loud...

Then, when she looked outside, the sky was grey, and rain was pounding on the ground.

Sophie trudged into the kitchen.

Sorry, we'll have
to go another day,

said Daddy.

Sophie started to cry.
Then, when she saw the picnic
basket all packed and ready,
she knocked it over, and it...

...CRASHED
to the floor.

Daddy showed Sophie how to clean up the mess
as the thunder rumbled even louder outside.

Can you make the same noise as the thunder?

Sophie stood up and

StomPed

her feet on the ground.

To her surprise, she felt a bit better, and she jumped around the kitchen with Daddy.

I've got an idea. Let's have our picnic in the living room!

He put Sophie's hat on her head, and she
took a bite of one of her fairy cakes.

It was the best
picnic ever!

The Clothes Thief

Harry loved his dressing-up box.

One day, he was
a fireman.

The next, he was
an astronaut.

Harry to
the rescue!

Blast off!

He even pretended
to be a cowboy as he
rode around the
living room.

Yee-haw!

He was so excited for his best friend's birthday party,
and he knew he'd have the best costume there.

Harry rummaged in the dressing-up box,
but it was no good. He had run out of costumes!

The next day, everyone was running late.

Where's my best shirt? I need to go to work,

said Mummy.

I can't find my shorts for the gym, either,

said Daddy.

I need my goggles for my swimming lesson!

called Harry's little sister.

They searched everywhere, but their missing things were nowhere to be found. There was a clothes thief in the house!

But someone wasn't missing anything.
Harry appeared at the top of the stairs,
and he was ready to go to the party!

"I've found the best costume ever! I'm going to the party as a swimming superhero!"

Everybody giggled. He really would have the best costume at the party after all.

My Magical Best Friend

The night before Mai's first day of nursery, Mummy tucked her into bed and kissed her on the forehead. Her bag was packed with her favourite toys and snacks, but Mai was still very nervous.

What if she didn't make any friends?
Mai tossed and turned all night.

When she woke up in the morning,
someone was standing beside her bed.

I'm Twinkle, your
new best friend!

Twinkle took Mai by the hand and before she knew it, they were flying through the air.

Then, they landed softly in the playground, and Mai waved goodbye to Twinkle as she went inside. After such an amazing adventure, Mai didn't feel nervous at all.

She couldn't wait to meet the other children at nursery, and she had fun eating her favourite snacks with her new friends at playtime.

But then, Mai watched the others playing outside.
They ran around and zoomed high on the swings.

When Mai sat at the top of the slide, she felt scared all
over again. She didn't want to slide down on her own.

Suddenly, Twinkle appeared.

So, they whizzed down the slide together,
and it didn't seem so scary any more.

Mai couldn't wait to play with all
her new friends the next day.

Ice Cream for Dinner

One sunny afternoon, Daddy and Ethan were playing at the park. When Ethan's tummy started to rumble, Daddy pointed to the ice cream van.

Ethan had never tried ice cream before, and Daddy
ordered him a cone with a strawberry swirl.

Mmm,
yummy!

It was so tasty that he finished
the whole thing all on his own.

Later that day, Daddy put a plate
of spaghetti on the table for dinner.

I made your favourite!

But Ethan crossed his arms and turned away.
Spaghetti wasn't his favourite any more. Ice cream was!

While everyone else tucked into their tasty dinner,
Ethan refused to eat a single bite.

Then, Daddy cleared
away all their plates
and replaced them with
bowls of ice cream!

You can only have ice cream for dessert if you finish your dinner.

So, Ethan grabbed his fork and gobbled up all his spaghetti until the plate was sparkling clean.

34

But for the first time that day,
Ethan didn't want any ice cream.
He felt so full, he thought he might burst.

35

Even Pirates Use the Potty

It was time for Emily to use the potty, but she didn't want to!

You're a big girl now!

said Mummy.

Emily stomped her feet and cried,

I'm going to wear nappies forever!

Mummy said that forever sounded like a very long time indeed.
She asked Emily if she would still wear nappies on a ship
if she sailed with a crew of swashbuckling pirates.

Even pirates
use the potty!

What if Emily became an astronaut? Would she still wear nappies in space, or when she walked on the moon?

Even astronauts use the potty!

Maybe Emily would live in a magical land and become a fairy-tale princess. Would she still wear nappies when she danced at the royal ball?

You can wear nappies forever and ever if you really want to.

Then, Mummy heard a TINKLE, TINKLE! Now, even Emily uses the potty!

I Want a Star

Maddie couldn't sleep. She sat up in bed and stared out of the window. The night sky was twinkling with thousands of tiny gleaming stars.

She jumped out of bed and ran downstairs.
Daddy came over and sat down with Maddie.

Maddie looked closer at the big round moon. It glowed in the darkness high above the houses on her street.

She imagined what it would be like to fly all the way to the moon on a shiny rocket. She could whizz past the stars and pick whichever one she liked.

Maddie would land on the moon and wave to everyone at home as they looked through their windows. Then, she'd drift back to Earth on a soft, fluffy cloud and fall fast asleep.

Daddy, I want a rocket! Then I can get the moon and a star all by myself.

Daddy laughed and took Maddie back upstairs.

Maybe one day, but not before bedtime.

Daddy closed the curtains, and Maddie climbed into bed. Suddenly, thousands of twinkling stars lit up her bedroom as Daddy turned on the night light.

Dream of all your big adventures,

he whispered as she fell asleep.